First published in 1982 by Grolier Enterprises, Inc.
This edition published by Scholastic Inc.,
90 Old Sherman Turnpike, Danbury, Connecticut 06816.

For information regarding permission, write to:
Disney Licensed Publishing, 114 Fifth Avenue, New York, New York 10011

ISBN 0-7172-6786-5

Printed in the U.S.A.
First printing, January 2003

Disney's Thumper

SCHOLASTIC INC.

New York   Toronto   London   Auckland   Sydney
Mexico City   New Delhi   Hong Kong   Buenos Aires

The forest was a peaceful place. Many families of animals made their homes there.

When the weather was nice, the young animals romped about and played together.

Among them was a young deer named Bambi. He
lived with his mother.

Bambi's father was the Great Prince of the Forest.
He was a big stag, and he was very brave.

Bambi's best friend
was a young rabbit
named Thumper.

One morning,
Thumper's mother told
her children, "We're
going to the meadow
to eat fresh clover for
breakfast."

"Hooray!" shouted Thumper. He jumped up onto a rock, startling some butterflies. As the beautiful creatures flitted away, Thumper tapped his foot on the rock.

Thump! Thump! Thump!

The little rabbit always did that when he was excited. That was why he was called Thumper.

Soon the rabbits reached the meadow. Many other
animal families were already there.

Thumper loved the sweet clover blossoms the best.
They looked like soft, fluffy rabbit tails. In fact, the
blossoms were all Thumper wanted to eat.

But his mother reminded him to eat the greens, too.
They would help him grow long ears and big feet.

After breakfast, Mother Rabbit told her children to stay nearby. She wanted them to be safe.

But Thumper didn't hear her. He had already gone hopping off to visit his friends.

First Thumper
found Friend Owl
perched in a tree.
"Whatcha doin' up there?"
Thumper asked.

"Hoo-o-o," Friend Owl hooted
sleepily. "Remember, Thumper, I
sleep during the day."

"Sorry, Friend Owl,"
Thumper said. "I'll come back
another time."

Next Thumper went to
find his friend Flower.
Thumper finally found
the young skunk playing
near a hollow log.

"Listen to this," Flower said to
Thumper. "Hello," Flower called
into the log. "Hel-l-o-o-o-o,"
Flower's voice echoed back.

Thumper laughed and jumped up onto the log. "Listen to this," he called. He began thumping his foot on the log.

Thump! Thump! Thump! The noise echoed through the forest.

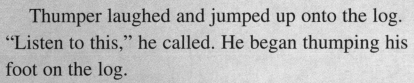

"That's wonderful," said Flower shyly. "How do you do that?"

"It's easy," replied Thumper. "See ya later, Flower," Thumper called as he jumped off the log. "I'm going to go find Bambi."

As he came into a thicket, Thumper found Bambi
resting with his mother.

"May we play together?" Thumper asked politely.

"Yes," said Bambi's mother. "But don't go too far
away," she warned.

"We won't," Thumper and Bambi promised as they
ran into the forest.

"Let's practice jumping," Thumper said to Bambi. "Practice makes perfect."

The young fawn nodded, and the two set off. As Thumper and Bambi raced into a clearing, the other animals scurried away.

Bambi easily jumped over a fallen log. But
Thumper did not.

"Whoops!" cried Thumper as he tripped and fell.

But Thumper wasn't hurt. Rolling over, he just laughed and laughed. "I think I need more practice," the little rabbit said.

"I'm glad you're not hurt," Bambi said.

"I never get hurt when I fall," Thumper giggled. "That's why fluffy tails are so great."

The two had fun in the forest until a voice called,
"Bambi." It was Bambi's mother. "It's time to rest," she
said. The young fawn headed off.

"See ya later, Bambi," Thumper said. But instead of
going back to his mother, he started chasing a butterfly.

Back at the meadow, Mother Rabbit noticed a storm was approaching. She called her children together. "Where's Thumper?" she wondered. "I told him to stay nearby. Now I can't see him anywhere."

"He's off exploring with his friends," one of Thumper's sisters said.

"You know he'll come back, Mama," another one added.

But Mother Rabbit was worried. "Wait here," she told her children. "I'm going to ask Friend Owl to help find Thumper."

"Friend Owl," called Mother Rabbit. "Have you seen Thumper?"

"He woke me earlier," Friend Owl said. "He's probably chasing some butterflies," he added as he tried to go back to sleep.

"But there's a thunderstorm coming," Mother Rabbit said. "Would you please try to find him?"

"Oh, all right," agreed Friend Owl. And off he flew. Suddenly a bolt of lightning crackled through the sky.

Friend Owl began searching the forest. Then off in the distance, he spotted fire! It was spreading quickly. "Oh, no!" Friend Owl exclaimed. "I must hurry and warn everyone!"

He rushed back
to Thumper's mother.
"I didn't find
Thumper," he told
her. "But a fire is
coming. Run to
the lake, where
you'll be safe."

"But we
can't leave without
Thumper!" Mother
Rabbit cried.

"Don't worry,"
comforted Friend Owl.
"I'll find him and bring
him to you." And off
he flew again.

"Hurry, children!" Mother Rabbit called.
She could already smell smoke from the fire.
"We must reach the lake."

"But what about Thumper?" they asked.
"Will he be all right?"

"Friend Owl will find him," their mother
hoped out loud.

Meanwhile, Thumper was happily playing with one of his butterfly friends. He didn't know a fire was spreading through the forest.

Friend Owl spotted Thumper just as another bolt of lightning struck nearby.

He quickly flew down to Thumper. "I'm so glad I found you," Friend Owl said.

"Why?" asked Thumper.

"Hurry, you must run to the lake," Friend Owl urged. "A fire is coming!"

"Where's my family?"
Thumper asked.

"They're safe at the
lake," Friend Owl told
him. "Come on,
Thumper, follow me."

"But I must warn
my friends first,"
thought Thumper.

So Thumper raced back
into the forest! He had to
find his friends.

Thumping loudly on a log, Thumper yelled, "Flower,
Flower, where are you?"

"What is it, Thumper?" Flower asked.

"Fire! Fire!" explained Thumper. "Run for the lake!"

"You come, too," said Flower.

"I will," Thumper said as he ran the other way.
"But first I must warn Bambi and his mother."

"All right, but please hurry," said Flower, and he
scurried off to the lake.

Thumper ran as fast as he could. Finally, he found Bambi sleeping next to his mother. "Wake up!" Thumper shouted.

"What is it, Thumper?" Bambi's mother asked.

"A fire is coming this way!" Thumper cried.

"We must go to the lake."

So Thumper, Bambi, and his mother raced
through the forest.

"Hurry, boys!" Bambi's mother said as the smoke
came closer.

Suddenly lightning hit a tall tree. As the tree
fell to the ground, it knocked Thumper into a hole.
Unfortunately, Bambi and his mother didn't see
what had happened.

As Bambi and his mother arrived at the lake, it
began to rain. Finally, the rain started to put out the fire.

"Thumper saved our lives!" Bambi said to
Thumper's mother.

"But where is he?" Mother Rabbit cried.

"Oh, no!" Bambi and his mother exclaimed when they realized Thumper wasn't with them.

"Try not to worry. I'll find him," said Friend Owl, and he headed back toward the forest.

When Friend Owl finally came back, he said, "I'm
so sorry. I couldn't find Thumper anywhere."

"Oh, no!" everyone cried.

All of the animals were sad. They thought they
would never see Thumper again.

"He was very brave to warn us," Bambi's mother
quietly added.

But Thumper was going to be all right. He was safe
in the hole! The fire hadn't touched him.

He had bumped his head when he fell into the hole
and was sound asleep. So Thumper hadn't heard
Friend Owl calling him.

All of a sudden rain
splashed on Thumper's
head and woke him up.

Thumper peeked out of the
hole—the fire was out!

"I have to let everyone know I'm all right."
Thumper jumped up onto a log and thumped
his foot. *Thump! Thump! Thump!* The sound
echoed through the forest.

Back at the lake, all the animals were very quiet, when suddenly Friend Owl shouted, "Wait, listen! I hear something."

Thump! Thump! Thump!

"That sounded like Thumper!" Mother Rabbit cried.
Minutes later, Thumper came racing around the lake.

Everyone was very happy to see him.
"Hooray for Thumper!" everyone shouted.

Thumper's mother was very proud of her son and lovingly patted him on the head. "I'm so thankful that you're all right, Thumper."

Thumper explained how he had fallen into a hole. "I didn't land on my tail that time," Thumper told Bambi. "I think I need more practice falling, too."

The young deer looked up at the brightening sky. "That's okay, Thumper. I think you are perfect the way you are."